Punia and the King of Sharks

A Hawaiian Folktale

ADAPTED BY LEE WARDLAW
PICTURES BY FELIPE DAVALOS

Dial Books for Young Readers · New York

For my nieces and nephews,
Maris, Jacob, and Galen Beck-Jaffurs,
Rosie and Isaac Fu Jaffurs,
with much aloha from Auntie Lee
L.W.

🦈 🦈 🦈 🦈 🦈 🦈 🦈 🦈

To children of all cultures
F. D.

Published by Dial Books for Young Readers
A Division of Penguin Books USA Inc.
375 Hudson Street
New York, New York 10014

Designed by Julie Rauer
Printed in Hong Kong
First Edition
1 3 5 7 9 10 8 6 4 2

Library of Congress Cataloging in Publication Data
Wardlaw, Lee, 1955—
Punia and the King of Sharks: a Hawaiian folktale/
adapted by Lee Wardlaw; pictures by Felipe Davalos.
p. cm.
Summary: Clever Punia, a Hawaiian fisherman's son, finds different ways
to trick the King of Sharks and take his tasty lobsters away from him.
ISBN 0-8037-1682-6 (trade).— ISBN 0-8037-1683-4 (lib. bdg.)
[1. Folklore—Hawaii.] I. Davalos, Felipe, ill. II. Title .
PZ8.1.W215Pu 1997 398.2'09969—dc20 [E] 93-43955 CIP AC

The art was prepared using ink and watercolor on Fabriano paper.

This adaptation of "Punia and the King of Sharks" was inspired by the
retelling of the ancient legend that appeared in Eric "Elika" Knudsen's 1946
book *Teller of Tales,* a collection of the spoken literature of old Hawaii.

A Glossary and Pronunciation Guide to Hawaiian Terms

hula (HOO-lah) a traditional Hawaiian dance performed by women whose graceful hand movements tell stories of famous Hawaiians and their great feats.

imu (EE-moo) an underground oven, used to steam the root of the taro plant.

kahuna (kah-HOO-nah) a sorcerer, priest, or medicine man. Also, an expert in any profession.

kapa (KAH-pah) known today as *tapa* (TAH-pah); a soft, strong cloth made from the inner bark of paper mulberry trees, used to make robes, clothes, and mats.

kukui (ku-KOO-ee) a Hawaiian nut; its oils were applied to ancient surfboards to keep them from drying out. Strings of kukui were also hung up and lit at night as a kind of torch.

lei (lay) a necklace or garland that is made from seeds, shells, ferns, berries, or flowers.

lūʻau (LOO-ow) a grand feast featuring entertainment such as a dance called the *hula*.

maile (MY-lay) a perfumed vine that was woven into crowns or necklaces for chiefs and kings. Today the vine is worn by the bride and groom in Hawaiian weddings.

manō (MAH-no) Hawaiian word for shark. The early islanders had 400,000 gods, including several shark gods.

papa heʻenalu (PAH-pah he-e-NAH-loo) Hawaiian term for surfboard. Surfboards originated in Hawaii over a thousand years ago and were used for transportation, entertainment, and fishing. Made of koa wood, they ranged from nine to fifteen feet and weighed one hundred to two hundred pounds when dry!

poi (poy) an Hawaiian food made from the root of the taro plant. Pounded and steamed to a thick paste, water is added to thin it.

Punia (poo-NEE-ah) a boy's name that means "head cold."

Please note that the same words often have different meanings depending on their pronunciation.

❥❥❥❥Beneath the rippling island water, near the shadows of a cave, lurked ten great sharks and the shark king who ruled them.

The sharks never swam far from shore, for the cave was filled with fat lobsters red as sunset, sweet as coconut.

"We must keep these lobsters for ourselves," said the King of Sharks, "and guard this cave from fishermen." And so they did, devouring anyone who ventured into the sea.

In a village nearby lived a boy named Punia. Once, his father had dared to fish in the lobster cave, only to be eaten by sharks. Now Punia and his mother had no one to fish for them. Day after day they ate only yams, which grew in the small garden behind their hut. And of course his mother served *poi*, the bland, thick paste Punia made by steaming taro roots in the *imu* and then pounding them with a rock.

Punia's mother never complained. But once in a while he heard her whisper, "Oh, if only we had a tender lobster to eat!" Punia said nothing, but as he licked the sticky poi from his fingers, his stomach rumbled in agreement.

One day Punia wandered along the jagged cliff above the lobster cave. He gazed into the clear, mint-blue sea and saw that the sharks were sleeping. Punia smiled, for suddenly he had a plan.

Leaning over the water, he spoke in a loud voice. "Oh-ho, look at this! The sharks are fast asleep! I, Punia, can dive into the waves and swim quick as a shrimp to the cave. I will scoop a fat lobster into each hand, and my mother and I shall have a tasty dinner tonight!"

"Did you hear that?" whispered the King of Sharks. He nudged the others awake and grinned, his sharp teeth glistening white as bone. "Let us race to the spot where Punia dives, then eat him as we ate his father."

Punia picked up a stone and heaved it as far as he could. *Splunk!*
The sharks raced toward the stone, thinking it was the boy. In a flash,
Punia dived into the unguarded cave, scooped a lobster into each
hand, and swam safely back to shore.

"Oh, King of Sharks," Punia taunted, "look what I have stolen
from you!" He held up the lobsters and shook his wet head, laughing.

"We have been tricked," the King of Sharks snapped in anger.
"How can this be?"

Punia laughed again and said, "Oh-ho, it was the shark with the flat nose who told me what to do!"

When the king heard this, he peered at each of his followers. Punia was right! One had a flat nose.

"So it was you, Flat Nose, who betrayed us!" the king said with a gnash of teeth. "I banish you from this cave forever!" With these words the King of Sharks, and the nine he ruled, gave Flat Nose a sharp nip on the tip of his tail and chased him out to sea.

Chuckling to himself, Punia set off for home, where he and his mother feasted that night on tasty lobster.

"You are clever, my son," his mother said, "but beware! You have angered the King of Sharks, and he will not be fooled so easily again."

Punia only smiled, for already he had another plan.

The next day Punia filled hollow gourds with thick poi.
He placed the gourds with care in a large basket, and carried it to the
cliffs above the lobster cave.

"Oh, King of Sharks!" Punia called. "I come to make amends for
the terrible trick I played. See what I bring: a magic feast prepared by
the *kahuna*, our sorcerer. One bite will make you fiercer than the sun
at noon. Two bites, and you shall grow stronger than four thousand
sharks, plus one."

"That is a generous gift to redeem such a small trick," the king replied, suspicious.

"Ah," said Punia, "but my mother and I are starving. I humbly ask, O great fish, that you allow me two more lobsters from your cave."

The king pretended to consider a moment. "Very well," he said at last. But to his followers he whispered, "Let us eat of the kahuna's magic. Then when Punia dives into the cave, we will eat him as we ate his father."

"Here is your feast!" cried Punia. With that he turned the basket upside down. Gourds tumbled into the sea. *Splunk! Splunk-Sploosh!* Instantly the sharks snapped at the gourds, crushing them with one crunch.

Punia dived into the water. The sharks tried to bite him, but their mouths would not open! Their teeth were stuck fast together with the gluelike poi. While they joggled their heads and bumped their snouts, Punia swam into the cave, scooping a fat lobster with each hand. The sharks raced after him. But by the time the poi dissolved and the sharks could open their jaws again, Punia had already swum safely back to shore.

"Tricked again!" the king roared. "How can this be?"

Punia laughed and said, "Oh-ho, it was the shark with the gray belly who told me what to do!"

The King of Sharks peered at each of his followers. Punia was right! One had a gray belly.

"You, Gray Belly, are a traitor! As punishment I banish you from this cave forever." With these words the King of Sharks, and the eight he ruled, nipped Gray Belly on the tip of his tail and chased him out to sea.

Punia chuckled and headed home, where he and his mother feasted on tasty lobster.

"You are clever, my son," his mother said, "but beware! Twice you have angered the king. His rage will make him ferocious. Only *Manō*, the great Shark God, could steal from him now."

Punia just smiled, for already he had another plan.

The next morning Punia took his father's *papa heʻenalu* from the canoe house. He oiled the wooden surfboard black with *kukui* nuts. Then on the underside he painted two blazing red eyes and a cruel mouth, and laid the board in the sun to dry. Later, board in tow, he

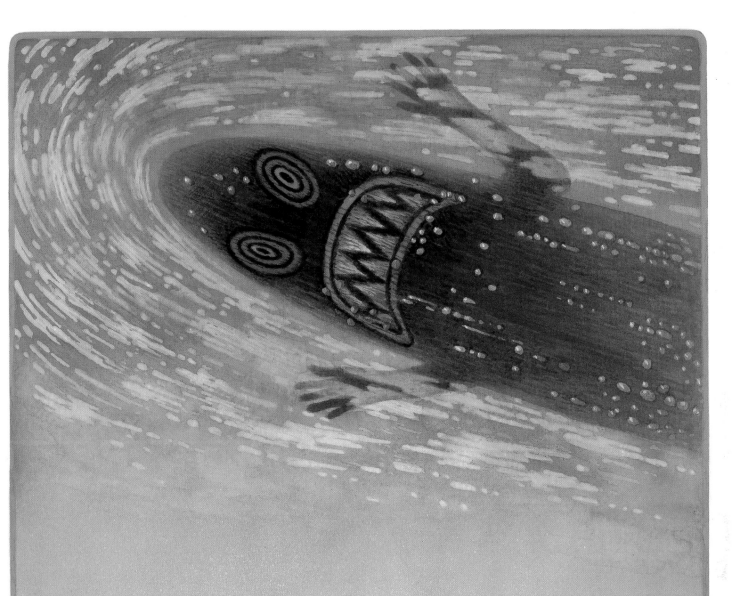

set off for the sea. The board was heavy and long, and Punia struggled, lugging and tugging his way down the grassy path. But at last he
reached the shore.

Punia gazed into the depths. The sharks were fast asleep. He paced
one hundred steps up the beach, away from the lobster cave. Then he
waded into the water, eased himself onto the board, and paddled,
swift but quiet, out to the distant waves. He caught the largest one
and leaped to his feet, balancing with arms outstretched like the
wings of a soaring bird. As the wave carried him closer to the lobster
cave, Punia cried in a booming voice: "I AM MANŌ, GOD OF
SHARKS! ALL WHO ARE LOYAL SHALL BOW BEFORE ME!"

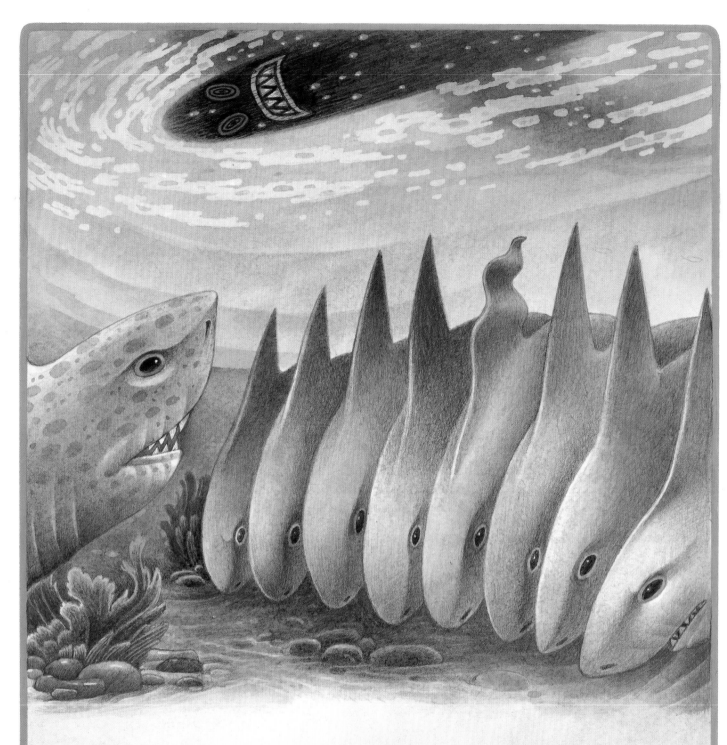

The king and his followers awoke and gazed up. A long shadow
with blazing red eyes and a cruel mouth was passing overhead.

"It is he! It is Manō!" cried the King of Sharks. "Bow down, I com-
mand you!"

Instantly each shark pointed its snout into the sandy bottom of
the sea.

At the same moment Punia dived off his board. He swam quick as a shrimp to the cave, scooped a fat lobster into each hand, and started back to shore.

Just then the king lifted his gaze to take a forbidden peek at the Shark God.

"That is not Manō!" he shouted. "See, he has no fins! No tail! And his eyes, they fade in water! It is the boy's doing!"

When Punia heard this, he began swimming faster, thrashing through the surf. The sharks saw him and gave chase. But Punia was too quick. He found the surfboard wedged against a rock, and still clutching the lobsters, scrambled atop it. As the king's mouth almost closed around the boy's foot, a wave caught the board and pushed Punia safely into shore.

"Tricked again!" the King of Sharks raged. "How can this be?"

Punia laughed and said, "Oh-ho, it was the shark with the crooked fin who told me what to do!"

"Traitors!" the king shouted, his tail swishing in anger. "I'm surrounded by traitors! As punishment I banish you *all* from this cave forever."

With these words the king nipped the tails of the sharks he ruled and chased them out to sea. When Punia whistled home with his lobsters that night, only the King of Sharks remained.

There is no one left to betray me, the king thought. Tomorrow I will not leave the mouth of this cave, no matter what I hear, no matter what I see. Then when Punia dives into the water, I shall eat him as I ate his father!

Early the next morning, before the sun crept up, Punia's mother watched as he set off to the cliff with several *kapa* cloths rolled under his arm.

"You are clever, my son," she said, "but beware! Three times you have angered the king. He feels no fear. Only the wrath of the volcanoes could frighten him now."

Punia smiled, for already he had another plan.

Working quietly while the king slept, Punia unrolled several kapa along the cliff's edge. Next he gathered as many stones as he could find, and piled them on top of the cloths. Finally he built a fire. Using sticks, he edged hot coals among the rocks. Then he shouted, "Flee! Flee for your life! The volcano erupts!"

With that Punia lifted the edge of a kapa, dumping stones and coals into the sea. Water churned and hissed. The shark king awoke to find rock raining around him. He darted away—then stopped. He ground his teeth. This is only the work of Punia, he thought. I shall not move.

Punia dumped another cloth into the sea, then another. "Flee!" he cried. "The volcano!" Rocks tumbled. Water boiled and steamed. Still the king did not move.

"He sleeps as deep as the volcano is high," Punia muttered. "Perhaps it will take the noise of one to awaken him." He glanced around, then hurried to a lava boulder teetering on the cliff's edge.

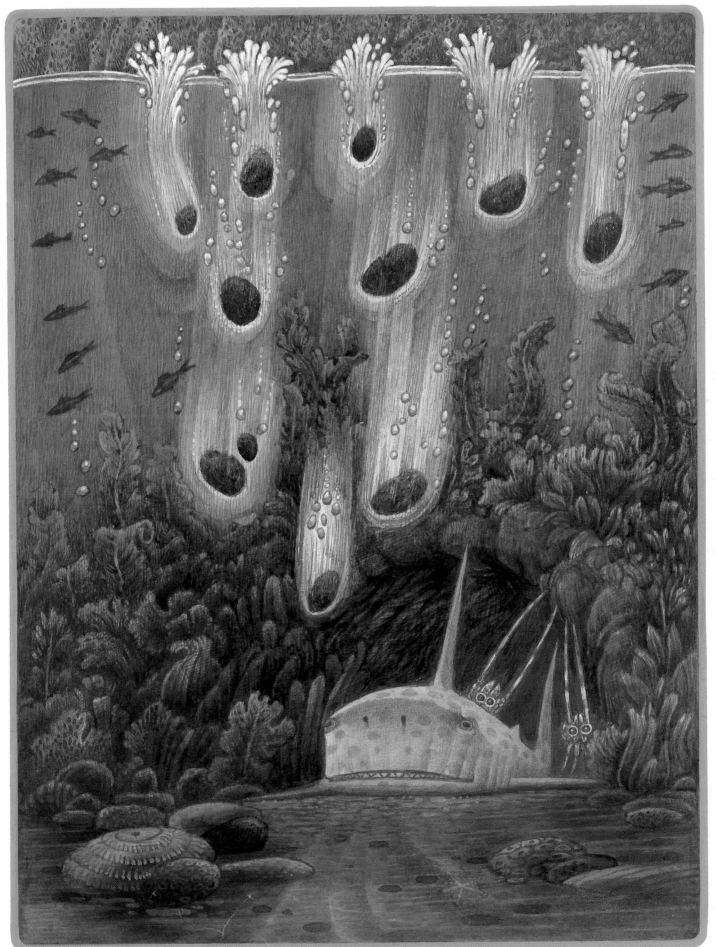

That will make a fine splash, he thought. Aloud, he shouted again, "The volcano!" Then with a grunt and a groan and a mighty push, Punia sent the boulder tumbling over the edge. But as he did so, he lost his balance. He flailed, snatching at the thick stalk of a banana tree, which grew out from the rocks. He dangled there above the sea, feet kicking, heart thumping like a drum.

"Oh-ho!" the King of Sharks called. "Who shall have the tasty dinner now?" He swam beneath Punia and poked his snout out of the water. "You cannot hang there forever, boy. Your arms are limp as seaweed, your fingers slippery as fish!" The shark chuckled, then opened his jaws and waited.

Frightened, Punia kicked again, trying to catch a foothold to scramble up the ledge. Too late! *Crack!* The stalk broke. Still clinging to it, Punia fell into the shark's mouth. Instantly he wedged the stalk between the king's teeth to keep the massive jaws from closing.

The King of Sharks thrashed about, trying to dislodge the stalk. He swam in frenzied circles, until Punia grew dizzy.

I must get out! Punia thought. But the water around them was inky and deep. Above them, waves dashed against a reef in a froth of white. If he tried to escape now, Punia feared he would drown.

Then Punia remembered how easily he had fooled the sharks. He had an idea. He knew it was his only chance.

In a shaky voice Punia cried, "Oh, if only the king would swim up into the breakers, I could ride safely into shore. But if he heads into the cove, I am doomed. For when I swim out of his mouth, he will surely bite me, and then I shall drown."

The King of Sharks heard this. He was very hungry, and so he streaked out of the depths, past the breakers, and into the cove. But the water there was too shallow for him. The shark stuck in the sand. Punia scrambled out of his mouth and scurried up the beach.

"Look!" Punia called to the villagers. "See who has come to visit us. He's not so fearsome now!"

The villagers crowded on the shore. The shark looked so foolish, flailing in the sand, his mouth propped open, that they began to laugh.

Snap! The shark's jaws finally broke the stalk. "How dare you!" he bellowed. "How dare you laugh—I am the King of Sharks!"

"No, you are the King of Sand Crabs," Punia replied.

The villagers laughed harder.

"Help me," the shark said, growing afraid. He struggled weakly under the hot sun. "Help me or I will die."

"That is what you deserve," Punia answered. "But I will help you under one condition. You must swim far out to sea and vow never to return."

"I give you my word!" croaked the shark. "Help me, please!"

Punia nodded. Then he asked the villagers to grab thick sticks and poles to push the shark back into the water. Ever watchful of the sharp teeth, the villagers did so. Without a word the former King of Sharks slipped quickly away, his fin disappearing at last in the distance.

The villagers cheered. "To Punia—the new King of Sharks!" They crowned him with a wreath of *maile* leaves and hung many *lei* around his neck, then hoisted Punia to their shoulders and carried him through the village. A *lū'au* was planned in his honor, where maidens danced a *hula*, which told the tale of his courageous deeds. And that night, and always after, the entire village feasted on sweet, tasty lobsters whenever they pleased.